Learn SCIENCE WITH MO
HABITATS

Paul Mason   Michael Buxton

Published in 2025 by Enslow Publishing, LLC
2544 Clinton Street
Buffalo, NY 14224

First published in Great Britain in 2023 by Wayland

Copyright © Hodder & Stoughton Limited, 2023

Design: Collaborate
Illustrations: Michael Buxton
Consultant: Peter Riley

All rights reserved. No part of this book may be reproduced in any form without permission in writing from the publisher, except by a reviewer.

Manufactured in the United States of America

CPSIA compliance information: Batch #CSENS25: For further information contact Enslow Publishing LLC, New York, New York at 1-800-398-2504.

Please visit our website, www.enslowpublishing.com. For a free color catalog of all our high-quality books, call toll free 1-800-398-2504 or fax 1-877-980-4454.

Cataloging-in-Publication Data

Names: Mason, Paul, author. | Buxton, Michael, illustrator.
Title: Habitats / by Paul Mason, illustrated by Michael Buxton.
Description: Buffalo, NY : Enslow Publishing, 2025. | Series: Learn science with Mo | Includes glossary.
Identifiers: ISBN 9781978538740 (pbk.) | ISBN 9781978538757 (library bound) | ISBN 9781978538764 (ebook)
Subjects: LCSH: Habitat (Ecology)--Juvenile literature. | Habitat conservation--Juvenile literature.
Classification: LCC QH541.14 M376 2025 | DDC 577--dc23

Find us on

Contents

Nature hikers	4
Habitats	6
Finding food	8
Microhabitats	10
Home habitats	12
Rory and the Arctic	14
Sid of the Sahara	16
Marcel's rainforest	18
Amy's mountain forest	20
Lily and the savanna	22
Ollie's coral reef	24
Dizzy and Dozy's river	26
Vacation time	28
Glossary	30
Books to read/Places to visit	31
Answers	32

The words in **bold** are in the glossary on page 30.

NATURE HIKERS

Mo is going on a nature hike with a walking group. They are looking for different animals and plants.

When they reach a pond, Dizzy and Dozy gaze into the water. What do they see?

Look, a dragonfly!

Surprised-looking fish!

And a snail!

And lots of plants.

Frog

It turns out that lots of plants and animals live together at the pond.

Next, the trail leads the explorers into some woods. The path is blocked by a log, so the friends roll it out of the way. They soon feel guilty, though …

The old log is home to lots of living things. They roll it back.

Earwig
Woodlouse
Fungi
Newt

BEING NATURE EXPLORERS IS GREAT! I WONDER WHERE ELSE WE COULD GO?

Why not go on vacation together to explore other places, Mo? You and your friends have relatives nearly everywhere. You could try to decide which ones to visit.

THAT'S A GOOD IDEA.

Thank you. Tell each other about what the different places are like, then decide whether everyone would enjoy it there.

Rory — Arctic
Sid — Desert
Marcel — Rainforest
Amy — Mountain forest
Lily — Savannah
Ollie — Coral reef
Dizzy and Dozy — River

HABITATS

WELCOME TO THE HABITAT EXPLORERS' CLUB!

The places the friends will explore on their hike are called **habitats**. The habitat of an animal or plant is the place where it normally lives or grows.

Most living things are **adapted** to live in their own habitat, but they might find it hard to survive somewhere different. The different habitat might be too hot, cold, wet or dry. It might be hard to find food or shelter.

Mo, can you match these animals with a habitat?
(The answers are at the end of the book.)

Mountain goat*

Jellyfish

Cheetah

Polar

Desert

River

*Easy one to start with.

Some plants and animals can survive in more than one kind of habitat.

The mountain goat could probably also survive on a savanna. It could not live in a river or the sea, though.

It's true. We're not good swimmers.

The penguin might be able to live beside a river — but it would not enjoy living up a mountain. It's not built for climbing.

Penguin

Wings are terrible at gripping

Short legs

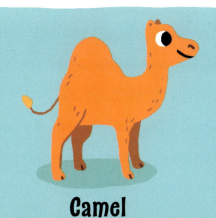

Camel

Penguin

Beaver

Savanna

Mountain

Ocean

FINDING FOOD

MUNCH! MUNCH! TUNA! MY FAVORITE.

Mo and friends are really hungry. It is a good thing they brought a packed lunch with them.

Imagine having to catch the tuna before you could eat it. Wild animals have to find food for themselves. We can show how this works in something called a **food chain**.

Food chain

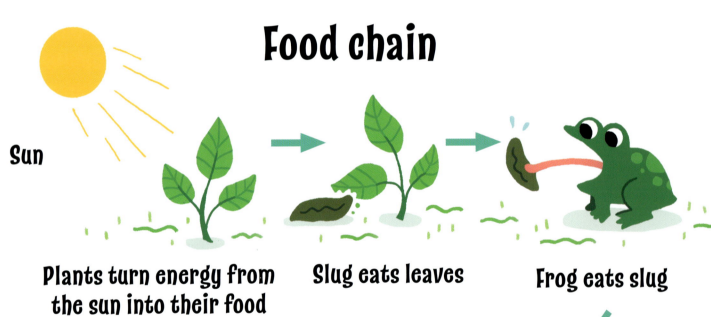

Sun

Plants turn energy from the sun into their food

Slug eats leaves

Frog eats slug

Bird of prey eats snake

Snake eats frog

Many animals are adapted to finding food in their own special habitat. For example, birds of prey are adapted to catch the food that is available.

Mo, see if you can match the birds of prey with their food:

1. Owl

Excellent hearing

Sees well in the dark

Fish

2. Merlin

Fast

Good at changing direction in the air

Mouse

3. Eagle

Strong talons to grip slippery things

Excellent eyesight

Small bird

OK – THAT SOUNDS LIKE FUN!

I can help.

Find out on page 32 whether you worked it out correctly.

MICROHABITATS

A microhabitat is a small area where plants and animals can find everything they need to survive.

Microhabitats are different from the area around them. Mo, remember the pond and the fallen log on pages 4 and 5? Those were microhabitats. How were they different from what was nearby?

OK! AROUND THE POND IT WAS DRY AND GRASSY ...
... BUT THE POND'S EDGES WERE WET AND MUDDY. IT HAD PLANTS AND LOTS OF INSECTS.

THE FOREST WAS DRY BUT UNDER THE LOG IT WAS DAMP. IT MUST HAVE BEEN DARK, TOO. AND THE WOOD WAS ROTTING.

Those are great answers, Mo!

THANK YOU. I DO TRY.

So what kinds of plants and animals live in those microhabitats?

AT THE POND ...
POND PLANTS GREW IN WATER. ANIMALS ATE OR LIVED IN THE PLANTS. ANIMALS THAT ATE INSECTS LIVED THERE, TOO.

UNDER THE LOG ...
THE ANIMALS WERE SMALL AND LIKED LIVING SOMEWHERE DAMP AND DARK. SOME OF THEM ATE ROTTING WOOD.

HOME HABITATS

Mo, Sid, and the others all live in the same place now – but their families originally came from lots of different habitats.

Each friend is adapted to live in their home habitat. Rory came from the Arctic, where it gets very cold.

Our furry coats kept us warm.

Sid's family lived in the dry desert.

We don't need to drink much.

Marcel originally came from the rainforest.

For life in the trees, our tails grip branches like an extra hand.

Amy's **ancestors** came from mountain forests.

It was cold and wet.
Our fur kept us warm.

Lily's family once lived on the savanna.

There were lions ...
... so we're all fast runners!

Dizzy and Dozy's parents lived by a river.

We ate a lot of fish.
Our sharp, pointed teeth grabbed them tight.

Ollie's grandpa came from a colorful coral reef.

Our skin changes color.
It helped us blend in and hide.

Each friend is going to tell Mo more about their home habitat. Mo will write down three things about it. Then the friends will use Mo's list to decide where to take their vacation.

RORY AND THE ARCTIC

Mo's cousin Rory comes from the Arctic. Maybe the friends' next nature exploration should be there? Tell us about it, Rory.

OK! In the Arctic, up near the North Pole, we only really have two **seasons**. They are winter and summer.

Winter

- Sun never rises or only shines for a short time
- Very cold
- Snow and ice everywhere

Snakes don't like the cold!

That sounds like a hard place to go on a nature hike, Rory!

The Arctic is really different in summer. It warms up (a bit), and plants and animals appear.

So, Mo, can you list three things about the Arctic to tell the others?

1. IT IS EITHER COLD (SUMMER) OR VERY COLD (WINTER).

2. NOT MANY PLANTS OR ANIMALS LIVE THERE ALL YEAR.

3. IT LOOKS REALLY PRETTY!

SID OF THE SAHARA

Sid's family originally came from a desert in Africa. What is that habitat like, Sid? What plants and animals live there?

The desert is beautiful — but very hot at midday! There is hardly any water.

So how do the animals survive, Sid?

Lots of us hide from the sun underground, then come out at night when it is cooler. Many animals are small. They have other adaptations, too.

Desert hedgehog:
Can last days without water

Fennec fox:
Big ears release lots of heat

Jerboa:
Nostrils close to keep out sand

Sid, your family comes from the world's hottest desert. Can any bigger animals (monsters, for example!) survive there?

Well, there are camels. They seem to like it!

Thick fur protects its skin from the sun

Thin fur elsewhere releases heat

Hardly sweats or pees to keep water inside its body

Wide feet are good for walking on sand

So, Mo, what are your three things to remember about the desert?

1. IT IS REALLY HOT IN THE DAY, BUT COOLER AT NIGHT.

2. THERE IS HARDLY ANY WATER.

3. ANIMALS SHELTER DURING THE DAY.

MARCEL'S RAINFOREST

It rains a lot in a rainforest. There are two kinds of rainforest. One is cool and the other is warm. Marcel's family came from a warm, **tropical** one – and Marcel thinks everyone should visit them!

> The rainforest has more plants and animals than any other habitat on Earth.

> Why are there so many plants and animals in the rainforest, Marcel?

> We have to start with a bit of science. Living things are divided into groups.

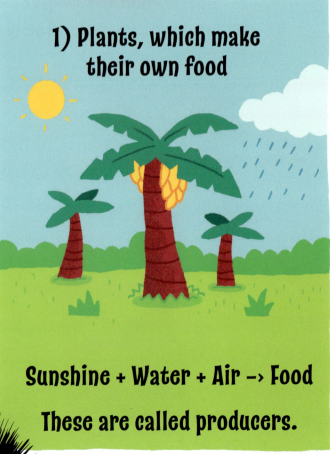

1) Plants, which make their own food

Sunshine + Water + Air → Food

These are called producers.

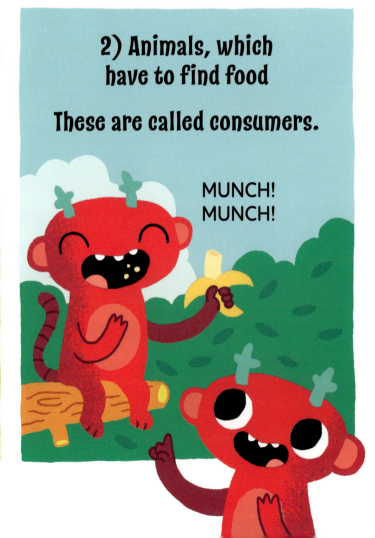

2) Animals, which have to find food

These are called consumers.

MUNCH! MUNCH!

In the rainforest, it is sunny and it rains a lot. Plants grow really quickly.

There are lots of plants for animals to eat ...

... and there are lots of animals for meat eaters to eat. This tapir had better watch out!

That does sound interesting, Marcel, and a bit dangerous! Mo, what are your notes about the rainforest?

1. IT RAINS A LOT SO BRING AN UMBRELLA!

2. THERE ARE MORE PLANTS AND ANIMALS TO SEE HERE THAN ANYWHERE ELSE.

3. IT IS HOT AS WELL AS WET IN TROPICAL RAINFORESTS.

AMY'S MOUNTAIN FOREST

Amy's ancestors used to live in forests on flat ground. Then those forests were cut down for wood and farmland. Her family moved to the mountains.

The mountains have steep sides. It often rains, and almost every day it is misty. It can be chilly, too. All kinds of rare animals live there:

1. Red panda

Wraps its tail around its face and tummy for warmth

Bushy tail

2. Takin

Long, shaggy coat

Strong legs for climbing

3. Snub-nosed monkey

Tiny, turned-up nose

Prevents frostbite (damage to skin from cold weather)

It sounds as though it would be a good idea for visitors to bring a waterproof coat. All that rain must be good for the plants.

So, Mo, what are your three things to remember about mountain forests?

LILY AND THE SAVANNA

Lily's family originally came from a habitat called the savanna. Lily, tell Mo why the savanna is interesting.

It is a **grassland** with some trees. The animals include tiny termites, slithery snakes, giant giraffes, and roaring lions.

Plants in the savanna

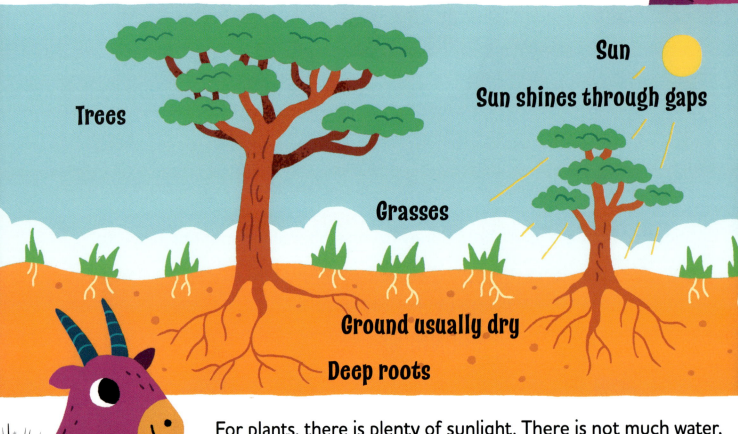

For plants, there is plenty of sunlight. There is not much water, though. The soil does not contain many **nutrients**. **Wildfires** often happen. Plants have to be tough to survive!

Wildfires and the savanna

Wildfires often burn the grasses and tree trunks. Sometimes trees are destroyed.

Animals flee.

No leaves

Blackened trunk

Burned ground

New leaves on trees

New grass grows from old roots and seeds

What are your three things to remember about the savanna habitat, Mo?

1. DON'T GO IN THE DRY SEASON, AS THERE MIGHT BE WILDFIRES.

2. TAKE SUNSCREEN: IT WILL BE SUNNY.

3. TAKE WATER BOTTLES: IT WILL BE DRY.

Coral reefs are home to many living things.
They are sometimes called the rainforests of the sea.

Water temperature: ideally 73–84°F (23–29°C)

Water is clear and lets sunlight reach underwater plants

Waves and currents bring nutrients to the reef

Larger fish eat reef plants or hunt smaller fish

Sharks are the top predators on the reef

Plants such as seagrass grow in the shallow, sunny water

Smaller fish hide from predators in the reef

So, Mo, what are the three things to remember about coral reefs?

1. REEFS FORM IN WARM, SALTY WATER.

2. LOTS OF COLORFUL PLANTS AND ANIMALS LIVE THERE.

3. YOU NEED TO BE ABLE TO SWIM TO EXPLORE A REEF.

DIZZY AND DOZY'S RIVER

Dizzy and Dozy don't like dry habitats, such as a desert or savanna. They prefer somewhere wetter.

We do! A lot wetter!

They normally live beside a river. They want to take their friends to see the plants and animals that live there. What is it like, Dizzy and Dozy?

We drew you a picture of the river our family came from. There are three main areas.

Zone 1: Riverbank

This is where our alligator cousins live. They hunt in the river and rest on the bank.

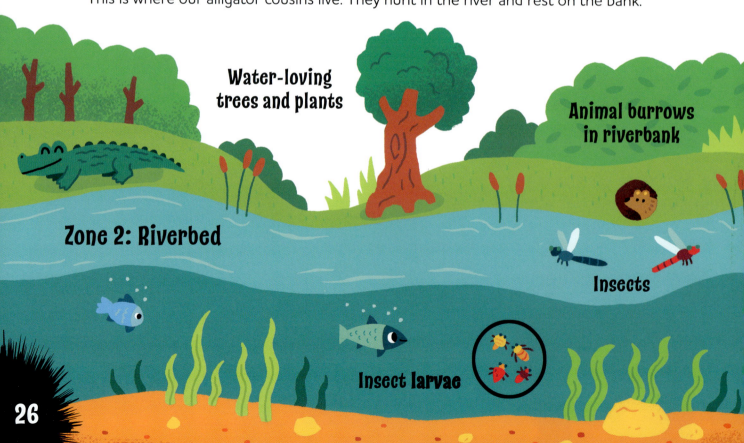

Water-loving trees and plants

Animal burrows in riverbank

Zone 2: Riverbed

Insects

Insect larvae

26

River water carries tiny pieces of soil and rock in it called sediment. When the water slows down, the rocks and soil sink and settle on the riverbed.

So, Mo, what are the three things to remember about river habitats?

1. THERE ARE THREE ZONES TO EXPLORE.
2. BRING INSECT REPELLENT, AS THERE ARE LOTS OF INSECTS.
3. LOTS OF PLANTS AND ANIMALS LIVE UNDERWATER.

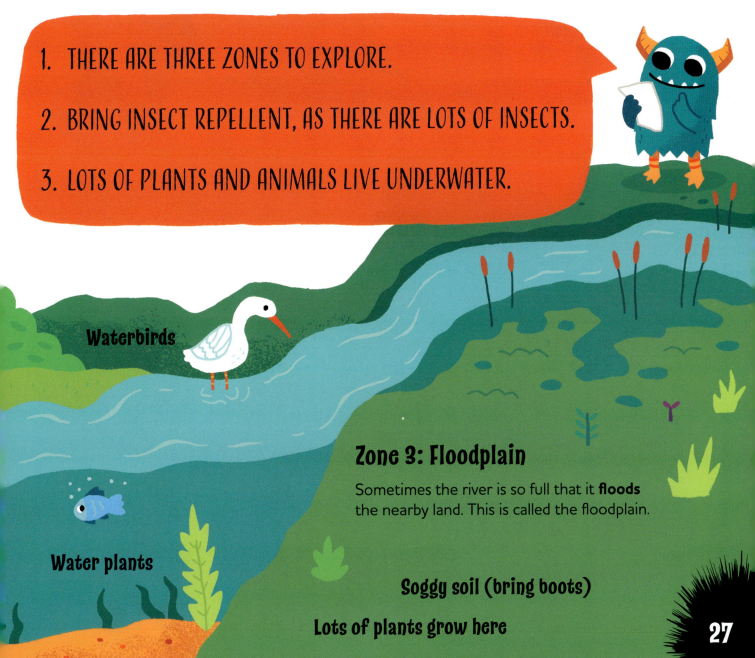

Zone 3: Floodplain

Sometimes the river is so full that it **floods** the nearby land. This is called the floodplain.

VACATION TIME

So, where should the friends go on a trip? It is time to look at Mo's notes and decide.

THE ARCTIC IN SPRING? IT'S STILL COLD, BUT THERE ARE PLANTS AND ANIMALS TO SEE.

Snakes hate the cold. I don't want to go there!

OK ... SO THE DESERT WOULD BE NICE AND HOT! OF COURSE, IT'S ALSO REALLY DRY.

I like wet, not dry!

THE RAINFOREST IS WET AND WARM! AND THERE ARE LOTS OF PLANTS AND ANIMALS TO SEE.

My fur would be too warm there.

THIS IS TRICKY! HOW ABOUT THE COOL, DAMP MOUNTAIN FOREST?

Crocodiles aren't really built for climbing mountains, though ...

Short legs

THE SAVANNA? THAT'S SUNNY AND WARM AND DRY.

Dry? Did you say dry?

OK, NOT THE SAVANNA. THE ONLY TROUBLE WITH OLLIE'S CORAL REEF IS THAT YOU HAVE TO LIVE UNDERWATER ...

We can't do that.

RIGHT, LAST ONE: DIZZY AND DOZY'S RIVER.

The river!

We can look for plants to eat.

We can hide and jump out at people!

I can climb trees.

I can sunbathe.

We can go fishing.

Although the team chose to visit the river habitat, all these habitats are amazing and precious. Many are at risk from human (and monster!) activity and pollution, so we need to protect them to make sure that they are safe for future generations of vacation-takers.

Glossary

adapted changed to become better at something (for example, hunting in a forest or surviving in very hot weather)

ancestor a member of your family who lived a long time ago

bamboo a tall grass with hard, hollow stems

bird of prey a bird that hunts other animals for food

coral reef a place where rock, coral, sand, or a combination of them is close to the sea's surface, creating a habitat filled with plants and animals

current a flow or movement of water all in the same direction

flood water covering an area of land where it would normally be dry

food chain a group of living things in which each one is food for the next one in the chain. There is an example of a food chain on page 8.

grassland a habitat where the most common plants are grasses. Grasslands are mostly dry.

habitat the natural home of a living thing, the place they are especially suited to living in

larva (plural **larvae)** the second life stage of an insect

mosquito a small, flying insect. Female mosquitoes feed on animals by sucking their blood.

moss a small green plant without roots that grows in damp places

nutrient something a living thing needs to survive, grow, and stay healthy

polar connected to the North or South Pole

season one part of the year when the weather and temperature is similar. Some parts of the world have four seasons: spring, summer, autumn, and winter, and some have two: a rainy season and a dry season.

tropical describes areas of the world on either side of the equator, an imaginary line that encircles Earth

wildfire a big fire that spreads quickly in dry conditions

Books to read

Outdoor Science: Habitats by Sonya Newland (Wayland, 2022)
Shows you how to explore your own habitat. Creepy-crawly safaris, pond explorations, rock-pool adventures, and more all feature in this thoroughly useful, hands-on outdoor-learning guide.

Science in Infographics: Habitats by John Richards and Ed Simkins (Wayland, 2021)
If you like statistics, numbers, charts and graphs – if you're fascinated by facts, basically – this is a great way to learn more about the world's habitats.

Body Bits: Eye-Popping Plant Parts and *Body Bits: Astounding Animal Body Facts* by Paul Mason, illustrations by Dave Smith (Wayland, 2021)
Leaning towards the horrifying and humorous, these books feature fascinating facts and funny cartoons that explain some of the amazing ways that plants and animals have adapted to their habitats.

Darwin's Tree of Life by Michael Bright, illustrated by Margaux Carpentier (Wayland, 2020)
Shows how the incredible range of different plants and animals on Earth developed. This is a beautiful book with plenty of fun facts: want to know why crabs run sideways, or why humans' brains are in their heads, not their feet? This is the place to find the answers.

Places to visit

American Museum of Natural History
200 Central Park West
New York, NY 10024

This museum has displays about all kinds of living things and their habitats. Don't miss the life-size model of a blue whale in the marine exhibit or the huge skeleton of a *T. Rex* in the dinosaur hall.

Smithsonian National Museum of Natural History
10th St. and Constitution Ave NW
Washington, D.C. 20560

This museum offers hand-on experiences to teach people about the natural world. Exhibits offer fascinating facts about biomes and habitats and the extraordinary animals that live in them, both today as well as millions of years ago..

Answers

Pages 6 and 7

Mountain goats live in **mountains** of course! Their strong legs help them climb up and down steep slopes.

Jellyfish live in the **ocean,** where they float around looking for small creatures to eat.

Cheetahs live on the **savanna,** where their speed helps them chase prey across the wide-open spaces. Their brown coats help them blend in with the brown grasses and plants.

Camels live in **deserts.** They have lots of adaptations for living in these dry places – you can see more on page 17.

Penguins live in **polar regions** around the South Pole. Their swimming skills help them catch fish to eat.

Beavers live in **rivers.** They use their strong teeth to cut down trees and build dams to live inside.

Page 9

To hear mice scurrying around you need good hearing. The owl hears well, so it would be able to hunt mice.

To catch other birds you need to be fast. The merlin flies fast, so it would be able to hunt small birds. (It is good at changing direction quickly, too, which would also be useful.)

Only the eagle is left. Sea eagles use their strong talons (claws) and good eyesight to catch fish.